To my sons, Peter, Michael and David, and their spontaneous natures
that have kept me young. Thanks boys.   D.D.

To my niece, Miranda   C.S.

Aladdin Paperbacks
An imprint of Simon & Schuster
Children's Publishing Division
1230 Avenue of the Americas, New York, NY 10020

10   9   8

Library of Congress Cataloging-in-Publication Data
DeLuise, Dom. Charlie the Caterpillar / by Dom DeLuise ; illustrated by Christopher Santoro.   p.   cm.   Summary: A caterpillar is rejected by various groups of
animals, until he achieves his beautiful wings and is able to befriend a similarly unhappy caterpillar.   [1. Caterpillars—Fiction.   2. Butterflies—Fiction.   3. Animals_
Fiction.   4. Friendship—Fiction.]   I. Santoro, Christopher, ill.   II. Title. PZ7.D3894Ch   1990   [E]—dc20   90-31557
ISBN: 0-671-69358-1 (HC)   ISBN: 0-671-79607-0 (pbk.)

DOM DE LUISE

CHARLIE
THE CATERPILLAR

ILLUSTRATED BY
CHRISTOPHER SANTORO

Aladdin Paperbacks

One day, one bright and sunny day,
Charlie the caterpillar was born.
   The world looked very, very big to Charlie…
because he was very, very small…
because he was just born.

Charlie soon found out how delicious green things tasted. As he was nibbling on a blade of grass, he could hear the wind whistling and the birds singing. He smiled. He was glad to be alive.

Charlie decided to set out and see the world,
so he looked to the left, and he looked to the right,
and then he went straight ahead.

Soon, Charlie saw two monkeys.
"Hi!" said Charlie. "What are you doing?"
"We're playing cards," they said.
"Oh!" said Charlie. "That sounds like fun.
Can I play, too?"
"No, you can't," said the monkeys.
"Why not?" asked Charlie.
"Because you're an ugly caterpillar.
Now giddadda here!"

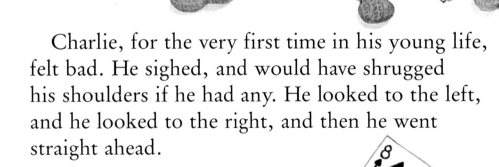

Charlie, for the very first time in his young life,
felt bad. He sighed, and would have shrugged
his shoulders if he had any. He looked to the left,
and he looked to the right, and then he went
straight ahead.

Pretty soon he saw two rabbits, hopping around.

"Hi!" said Charlie. "What are you doing?"

"We're playing tennis," they said.

"Oh!" said Charlie. "That looks like fun.
Can I play, too?"

"No, you can't," said the rabbits.

"Why not?" asked Charlie.

"Because you're an ugly caterpillar,
and we don't play with ugly caterpillars.

Now giddadda here!"

Now, for the second time in his young life, Charlie
felt bad, very bad. His feelings were hurt.

"What is ugly?" wondered Charlie. He didn't *feel* ugly.
He looked to the left, and he looked to the right,
and then he went straight ahead.

Just then, Charlie saw two mice playing
miniature golf. (These mice were so small,
they *had* to play miniature golf.)

"Hi!" said Charlie. "What are you doing?"

"We're playing golf," they answered.

"Oh!" said Charlie. That *really* looks like fun.
Can I play too?"

"No, you can't," said the mice.

"Why not?" asked Charlie.

"Because you're an ugly caterpillar, and we
really don't play with ugly caterpillars.

Now, giddadda here!"

Charlie, for the third time in his now not-so-young life,
felt very, very bad. In fact, Charlie started to feel ugly.

No one wanted to play with him. So Charlie looked to
the left, and he looked to the right, and then he started to cry.

Charlie wanted to be alone. He climbed up a tree, and snuggled up to a small branch. He felt a little cold, so he went like this, and he went like that, and he went like this, and he went like that, and before he knew it, he had spun himself a warm and wonderful cocoon.

Charlie was very sad about
that "ugly" business.
"Why can't I have a friend?"
he wondered.
Charlie was so tired from
making the cocoon, that he
decided to take a nap.

All of a sudden, snow began to fall
and to cover everything with white.
Winter had come, but Charlie was nice
and warm in his comfortable cocoon.
Charlie dreamed that he had a
best friend, and that they laughed
and had fun together.

After a while, the grass began to grow, the flowers began to bloom, and the birds began to have a party in the sky. Spring had come and, somehow, Charlie knew it was time to wake up.

He yawned and stretched and then—oh my goodness—

POP! POP!

Charlie looked to the left, and he looked to the right, and oh!—he had wings! Beautiful wings! Butterfly wings! Charlie had become a beautiful butterfly!

Charlie fluttered his wings, and guess what? He flew up, up and up! He laughed as he soared past the birds having a party in the sky. Charlie was flying high when he came upon the monkeys who were still playing cards.

"Oh, please come and play with us," begged the monkeys.
"Why?" asked Charlie.
"Because you're a beautiful butterfly," they answered.
"No thanks," said Charlie, smiling.
"I gotta giddadda here!"

He zoomed up and away. The monkeys jumped back, looking miserable.
"Serves them right," thought Charlie.

He did a couple of loop-the-loops, and then he came across the rabbits at their tennis game.

"Oh please," said the rabbits. "Won't you come and play with us?"

"Why?" asked Charlie.

"Because you're such a beautiful butterfly!" they answered.

"Not on your life," said Charlie.

"Now I gotta giddadda here!"

Then off he flew, leaving the rabbits looking very downhearted.

"Serves them right," thought Charlie.

He circled around for a while, and then he saw the mice playing miniature golf.

"Please, pretty please," pleaded the mice. "Do come and play with us!"

"Why?" asked Charlie.

"Because you're *really* such a beautiful butterfly," they answered.

"Sorry, not today," said Charlie. "I *really* have better things to do.

Now I gotta giddadda here!"

Then off he soared, leaving the mice looking pitiful. "Serves them right," thought Charlie.

They all wanted to be his friend because he was now a beautiful butterfly. They didn't know that he was Charlie, the ugly caterpillar.

"If they want to be my friends just because
of my beautiful wings, they can't be *real* friends,"
thought Charlie as he fluttered in the spring sunshine.
Just then, Charlie heard someone crying.

It was Katie the Caterpillar. Charlie came closer.

"Why are you crying?" he asked.

"Because no one will play with me. No one wants to be my friend," cried Katie, "because I'm an ugly caterpillar."

"I'll play with you," said Charlie, with a wink and a smile. "I'll be your friend."

"You will?" said Katie the Caterpillar. "Whoopie!"

Then Charlie took Katie aside and told her all about becoming a butterfly.

From that day on, Charlie and Katie played cards and tennis and even miniature golf together. They laughed and had a good time, just like in Charlie's dream. Katie was happy, and Charlie was *very* happy. He had finally found a friend…a real friend…a best friend.